To
Be...

From:

Nonnie

Easter
Sunday

2018

For:

. . . .

From:

. . . .

Date:

. . . .

My Little Prayers

Compiled by Brenda Ward

Illustrations by Diane Le Feyer

A Division of Thomas Nelson Publishers

Published in Nashville, Tennessee, by Tommy Nelson. Tommy Nelson is an imprint of Thomas Nelson. Thomas Nelson is a registered trademark of HarperCollins Christian Publishing, Inc.

Tommy Nelson titles may be purchased in bulk for educational, business, fund-raising, or sales promotional use. For information, please e-mail SpecialMarkets@ThomasNelson.com.

Unless otherwise noted, Scripture quotations are taken from the International Children's Bible®. Copyright © 1986, 1988, 1999 by Thomas Nelson. Used by permission. All rights reserved.

Scripture quotations marked KJV are taken from the King James Version. Public domain.

ISBN-13: 978-0-7180-4019-2

Library of Congress Control Number: 2015955650

Printed in China
16 17 18 19 20 DSC 6 5 4 3 2 1

Mfr: DSC / Shenzhen, China / May 2016 / PO # 9378640

Contents

· · · · · · · · ·

The Lord is all I need. He takes care of me.

Psalm 16:5

My Day

Day by day, dear Lord, of Thee
Three things I pray:
To see Thee more clearly,
Love Thee more dearly,
Follow Thee more nearly,
Day by day.

St. Richard of Chichester

Thank You, God, for
this new day,
In my school, at work and play.
Please be with me all day long,
In every story, game, and song.
May all the happy
things we do
Make You, our Father,
happy too.

Author Unknown

For this new morning with its
     light,
For rest and shelter of the night,
For health and food,
For love and friends,
For every gift Your
     goodness sends,
We thank You, gracious
     Lord. Amen.

                              Traditional

All for You, dear God.
Everything I do,
Or think,
Or say,
The whole day long.
Help me to be good.

Author Unknown

When the weather is wet,
We must not fret.
When the weather is cold,
We must not scold.
When the weather is warm,
We must not storm.
Be thankful together,
Whatever the weather.

Author Unknown

He gives food to every living creature. His love continues forever.

Psalm 136:25

My Mealtime

God is great.
God is good.
Let us thank Him for our food.

Traditional

*Thank You for the world so
    sweet,
Thank You for the food we eat,
Thank You for the
    birds that sing,
Thank You, God, for everything!*

E. Rutter Leatham

The Lord is good to me,
And so I thank the Lord
For giving me the things I need:
The sun, the rain, and
    the apple seed!
The Lord is good to me.

Traditional

God, we thank You for this
    food,
For rest and home and
    all things good;
For wind and rain and
    sun above,
But most of all for
    those we love.

Maryleona Frost

I go to bed and sleep in peace. Lord, only you keep me safe.

Psalm 4:8

My Bedtime

Now I lay me down to sleep.
I pray Thee, Lord, my
soul to keep.
Your love be with me
through the night
And wake me with the
morning light.

Traditional

Lord, keep us safe this night,
Secure from all our fears.
May angels guard us
*   while we sleep,*
Till morning light appears.

Traditional

Lord, with Your praise we drop
  off to sleep.
Carry us through the night;
Make us fresh for the morning.
Hallelujah for the day!
And blessing for the night!
  A Ghanaian Fisherman's Prayer

*Father, we thank You for the
     night,
And for the pleasant
     morning light,
For rest and food and
     loving care,
And all that makes
     the day so fair.*

*Help us to do the things we
     should,
To be to others kind and good;
In all we do and all we say,
To grow more loving every day.*

Author Unknown

Children, obey your parents the way the Lord wants. This is the right thing to do.

Ephesians 6:1

My Family and Friends

God bless all those that I love.
God bless all those
*   that love me.*
God bless all those that love
Those that I love, and all those
That love those that love me.

New England Sampler

Thank You for my parents, Lord,
And all the fun we've had.
There's no time I love better
Than with my mom and dad.

Help me, Lord, to always know
The many ways they care.
For toys and snacks and
    big bear hugs
And always being there.

When I grow up, I want to be
Just like my parents too.
Because they make
    me feel so great
And love me just like You.

Beth Burt

May the road rise to meet you.
May the wind be always
at your back.
May the sun shine warm
on your face,
The rains fall softly on
your fields;
And until we meet again,
May God hold you in the
palm of His hand.

Traditional, Irish

Dear Lord,
Thank You for my
grandparents.
They always have time to read
to me or play games.
They like to tickle and
play and laugh.
And they like ice cream and
going to the park too.
Mostly though, God,
they love me.
Please take care of them, Lord.
I think they must be
a lot like You.

Author Unknown

*Our family's big, our house is
    small;
We're crowded as can be.
But, Father, there's a lot of love
That's shared here happily.*

*I love my mom and daddy too;
They keep me safe each day.
But thanks for brothers
    and sisters, Lord;
They have more time to play.*
                Mary Hollingsworth

> *The Lord is my shepherd.*
> *I have everything I need.*
>
> Psalm 23:1

My Favorite Things

Please give me what I ask,
*   dear Lord,*
If You'd be glad about it.
But if You think it's not for me,
Please help me do without it.
Traditional

Dear Father,
Hear and bless
Thy beasts and singing birds.
And guard with tenderness
Small things that have
      no words.

Author Unknown

For rosy apples, juicy plums,
And honey from the bees,
We thank You, heavenly
Father God,
For such good gifts as these.

Author Unknown

The beautiful bright sunshine
That smiles on all below,
The waving trees, the
*   cool, soft breeze,*
The rippling streams that flow,
The shadows on the hillsides,
The many tinted flowers,
With greatest love and
*   tender care*
You made this earth of ours.

Author Unknown

When I am afraid, I will trust you.

Psalm 56:3

My Feelings

Dear Lord,
Thank You that I am
    sometimes strong,
Help me when I am still weak;
Thank You that I am
    sometimes wise,
Help me when I am still foolish;
Thank You that I have
    sometimes done well,
Forgive me the times I
    have failed You;
And teach me to serve
    You and Your world
With love and faith and truth,
With hope and grace and
    good humor. Amen.

A Swaledale Parish Prayer

I feel happy, Jesus!
I am happy when I laugh with
friends, or hold a puppy.
I feel happy eating ice cream,
or listening to a story.
I feel happy when someone
says, "I love you."
Lord, I am happy because
I belong to You!
That is the best thing of all
to be happy about!

Sheryl Crawford

Dear God, my friend is moving,
and I'm so sad.
We've had so much fun
together, and I don't
want her to move.
Please help her to find new
friends where she's going
so she won't be lonely.
And help me to make
new friends too.
Thank You, Jesus, for being
my best friend.

Author Unknown

Dear God, be good to me.
The sea is so wide,
And my boat is so small.
The Breton Fisherman's Prayer

*Jesus, someone I care for lives
     with You now.
I feel very sad because that
     person is not here.
Sometimes I cry . . . to let
     the sadness out.
Lord, You say that people who
     live with You are happy.
In heaven, there are angels
     and friends and family.
Jesus, please help me to
     remember that someday
     we will be together again
     with the ones we love . . .
And we will live forever
     with You in heaven!*

Sheryl Crawford

This is the day that the Lord has made. Let us rejoice and be glad today!

Psalm 118:24

My Special Days

My Birthday

Dear Lord, I am happy today
because it is my birthday!
I was born on a day like today.
It was a great day for
my family, one they
could never forget.
Thank You for fun things,
like cake and candles,
for family and friends
and presents and
birthday cards.
But most of all, Lord, thank
You for giving me life!

Sheryl Crawford

Christmas

What can I give Him,
Poor as I am?
If I were a shepherd,
I would bring Him a lamb.
If I were a wise man,
I would do my part.
But what can I give Him?
Give Him my heart.

Christina G. Rossetti

Christmas

Away in a manger, no crib for
*   a bed,*
The little Lord Jesus laid
*   down His sweet head;*
The stars in the sky looked
*   down where He lay,*
The little Lord Jesus,
*   asleep on the hay.*

Be near me, Lord Jesus; I ask
*   Thee to stay*
Close by me forever, and
*   love me, I pray;*
Bless all the dear children
*   in Thy tender care,*
Prepare us for heaven, to
*   live with Thee there.*

Martin Luther

Easter

He is Lord,
He is Lord!
He is risen from the dead
     and He is Lord!
Every knee shall bow;
Every tongue confess,
that Jesus Christ is Lord.

Traditional

The Lord listens when I pray to him.

Psalm 4:3

My Time with God

Two little eyes to look to God;
Two little ears to hear His Word;
Two little feet to walk
*   in His ways;*
Two little lips to sing His praise;
Two little hands to do His will;
And one little heart to
*   love Him still.*

Traditional

All things bright and beautiful,
All creatures great and small,
All things wise and wonderful,
The Lord God made them all.

He gave us eyes to see them,
And lips that we might tell
How great is God Almighty,
Who has made all things well!

Carl Frances Alexander

God be in my head
And in my understanding.
God be in mine eyes
And in my looking.
God be in my mouth
And in my speaking.
God be in my heart
And in my thinking.

Author Unknown

The Lord's Prayer

Our Father which art in heaven,
hallowed be thy name.
Thy kingdom come,
Thy will be done in earth,
as it is in heaven.
Give us this day our
daily bread.
And forgive us our debts, as
we forgive our debtors.
And lead us not into
temptation, but
deliver us from evil:
For thine is the kingdom,
and the power, and the
glory, for ever. Amen.

Matthew 6:9–13 KJV